CHITRA

RABINDRANATH TAGORE

GYAN

Published by

GYAN

Gyan Publishing House
5, Ansari Road
Daryaganj, New Delhi-110002
Phone: 011-47034999, 9811692060
E-mail: books@gyanbooks.com

Distribution Network
gyanbooks.com
India, USA, Canada, UK, Australia

ISBN: 978-93-6780-044-7 (HB)

First Published, 1913

2nd Impression 2025

Printed at: Gyan Press, Delhi.

CHITRA
Author: RABINDRANATH TAGORE

CHITRA

CHITRA

BY

RABINDRANATH TAGORE

A PLAY IN ONE ACT

INDIAN EDITION

MACMILLAN AND CO., LIMITED
ST. MARTIN'S STREET, LONDON
1953

TO

MRS. WILLIAM VAUGHN MOODY

PREFACE

THIS lyrical drama was written about twenty-five years ago. It is based on the following story from the Mahabharata.

In the course of his wanderings, in fulfilment of a vow of penance, Arjuna came to Manipur. There he saw Chitrāngadā, the beautiful daughter of Chitravāhana, the king of the country. Smitten with her charms, he asked the king for the hand of his daughter in marriage. Chitravāhana asked him who he was, and learning that he was Arjuna the Pandava, told him that Prabhanjana, one of his ancestors in the kingly line of Manipur, had long been childless. In order to obtain an heir, he performed severe penances. Pleased with these austerities, the god Shiva gave him this boon, that he and his successors should each have one child. It so happened that the promised child had invariably been a son. He, Chitravāhana, was the first to have only a daughter Chitrāngadā to perpetuate the race. He had, therefore, always treated her as a son and had made her his heir. Continuing, the king said:

"The one son that will be born to her must be the perpetuator of my race. That son will be the price that I shall demand for this marriage. You can take her, if you like, on this condition."

Arjuna promised and took Chitrāngadā to wife, and lived in her father's capital for three years. When a son was born to them, he embraced her with affection, and taking leave of her and her father, set out again on his travels.

THE CHARACTERS

GODS :

MADANA (Eros).

VASANTA (Lycoris).

MORTALS :

CHITRA, daughter of the King of Manipur.

ARJUNA, a prince of the house of the Kurus. He is of the Kshatriya or "warrior caste," and during the action is living as a Hermit retired in the forest.

VILLAGERS from an outlying district of Manipur.

NOTE.—The dramatic poem "Chitra" has been performed in India without scenery—the actors being surrounded by the audience. Proposals for its production here having been made to the author, he went through this translation and provided stage directions, but wished these omitted if it were printed as a book.

SCENE I

Chitra

ART thou the god with the five darts, the Lord of Love?

Madana

I am he who was the first born in the heart of the Creator. I bind in bonds of pain and bliss the lives of men and women!

Chitra

I know, I know what that pain is and those bonds.—And who art thou, my lord?

Vasanta

I am his friend—Vasanta—the King of the Seasons. Death and decrepitude would wear the world to the bone but that I follow them and constantly attack them. I am Eternal Youth.

Chitra

I bow to thee, Lord Vasanta.

Madana

But what stern vow is thine, fair stranger? Why dost thou wither thy fresh youth with penance and mortification? Such a sacrifice is not fit for the worship of love. Who art thou and what is thy prayer?

Chitra

I am Chitra, the daughter of the kingly house of Manipur. With godlike grace Lord Shiva promised to my royal grandsire an unbroken line of male descent. Nevertheless, the divine word proved powerless to change the spark of life in my mother's womb—

so invincible was my nature, woman though I be.

Madana

I know, that is why thy father brings thee up as his son. He has taught thee the use of the bow and all the duties of a king.

Chitra

Yes, that is why I am dressed in man's attire and have left the seclusion of a woman's chamber. I know no feminine wiles for winning hearts. My hands are strong to bend the bow, but I have never learnt Cupid's archery, the play of eyes.

Madana

That requires no schooling, fair one. The eye does its work untaught, and he knows how well, who is struck in the heart.

Chitra

One day in search of game I roved alone to the forest on the bank of the Purna river. Tying my horse to a tree trunk I entered a dense thicket on the track of a deer. I found a narrow sinuous path meandering through the dusk of the entangled boughs, the foliage vibrated with the chirping of crickets, when of a sudden I came upon a man lying on a bed of dried leaves, across my path. I asked him haughtily to move aside, but he heeded not. Then with the sharp end of my bow I pricked him in contempt. Instantly he leapt up with straight, tall limbs, like a sudden tongue of fire from a heap of ashes. An amused smile flickered round the corners of his mouth, perhaps at the sight of my boyish countenance. Then for the first time in my life I felt myself a woman, and knew that a man was before me.

Madana

At the auspicious hour I teach the man and the woman this supreme lesson to know themselves. What happened after that ?

Chitra

With fear and wonder I asked him "Who are you ?" "I am Arjuna," he said, "of the great Kuru clan." I stood petrified like a statue, and forgot to do him obeisance. Was this indeed Arjuna, the one great idol of my dreams ! Yes, I had long ago heard how he had vowed a twelve-years' celibacy. Many a day my young ambition had spurred me on to break my lance with him, to challenge him in disguise to single combat, and prove my skill in arms against him.

Ah, foolish heart, whither fled thy presumption? Could I but exchange my youth with all its aspirations for the clod of earth under his feet, I should deem it a most precious grace. I know not in what whirlpool of thought I was lost, when suddenly I saw him vanish through the trees. O foolish woman, neither didst thou greet him, nor speak a word, nor beg forgiveness, but stoodest like a barbarian boor while he contemptuously walked away! . . . Next morning I laid aside my man's clothing. I donned bracelets, anklets, waist-chain, and a gown of purple red silk. The unaccustomed dress clung about my shrinking shame; but I hastened on my quest, and found Arjuna in the forest temple of Shiva.

Madana

Tell me the story to the end. I am

the heart-born god, and I understand the mystery of these impulses.

Chitra

Only vaguely can I remember what things I said, and what answer I got. Do not ask me to tell you all. Shame fell on me like a thunderbolt, yet could not break me to pieces, so utterly hard, so like a man am I. His last words as I walked home pricked my ears like red-hot needles. "I have taken the vow of celibacy. I am not fit to be thy husband!" Oh, the vow of a man! Surely thou knowest, thou god of love, that unnumbered saints and sages have surrendered the merits of their life-long penance at the feet of a woman. I broke my bow in two and burnt my arrows in the fire. I hated my strong, lithe arm, scored by drawing the bow-string. O Love, god Love, thou hast laid low in the dust the vain pride of my manlike strength; and all my man's training lies crushed under thy feet. Now teach me thy lessons; give me the power of the weak and the weapon of the unarmed hand.

Madana

I will be thy friend. I will bring the world-conquering Arjuna a captive before thee, to accept his rebellion's sentence at thy hand.

Chitra

Had I but the time needed, I could win his heart by slow degrees, and ask no help of the gods. I would stand by his side as a comrade, drive the fierce horses of his war-chariot, attend him in the pleasures of the chase, keep guard at night at the entrance of his tent, and help him in all the great duties of a Kshatriya, rescuing the weak, and meting out justice where it is due. Surely at last the day would have come for him to look at me and wonder, "What boy is this? Has one of my slaves in a former life followed me like my good deeds into this?" I am not the woman who nourishes her despair in lonely silence, feeding it with nightly tears and covering it with the daily patient smile, a widow from her birth. The flower of my desire shall never drop into the dust before it has ripened to fruit. But it is the labour of a life-time to make one's true self known and honoured. Therefore I have come to thy door, thou world-vanquishing Love, and thou, *Vasanta*, youthful Lord of the Seasons, take from my young body this primal injustice, an unattractive plainness. For a single day make me superbly beautiful, even as beautiful as was the sudden blooming of love in my heart. Give me but one brief day of perfect beauty, and I will answer for the days that follow.

Madana

Lady, I grant thy prayer.

Vasanta

Not for the short span of a day, but for one whole year the charm of spring blossoms shall nestle round thy limbs.

SCENE II

Arjuna

WAS I dreaming or was what I saw by the lake truly there? Sitting on the mossy turf, I mused over bygone years in the sloping shadows of the evening, when slowly there came out from the folding darkness of foliage an apparition of beauty in the perfect form of a woman, and stood on a white slab of stone at the water's brink. It seemed that the heart of the earth must heave in joy under her bare white feet. Methought the vague veilings of her body should melt in ecstasy into air as the golden mist of dawn melts from off the snowy peak of the eastern hill. She bowed herself above the shining mirror of the lake and saw the reflection of her face. She started up in awe and stood still; then smiled, and with a careless sweep of her left arm unloosed her hair and let it trail on the earth at her feet. She bared her bosom and looked at her arms, so flawlessly modelled, and instinct with an exquisite caress. Bending her head she saw the sweet blossoming of her youth and the tender bloom and blush of her skin. She beamed with a glad surprise. So, if the white lotus bud on opening her eyes in the morning were to arch her neck and see her shadow in the water, would she wonder at herself the live-long day. But a moment after the smile passed from her face and a shade of sadness crept into her eyes. She bound up her tresses, drew her veil over her arms, and sighing slowly, walked away like a beauteous evening fading into the night. To me the supreme fulfilment of desire seemed to have been revealed in a flash and then to have vanished. . . . But who is it that pushes the door?

Enter CHITRA, *dressed as a woman.*

Ah! it is she. Quiet, my heart! Fear me not, lady! I am a Kshatriya.

Chitra

Honoured sir, you are my guest. I live in this temple. I know not in what way I can show you hospitality.

Arjuna

Fair lady, the very sight of you is indeed the highest hospitality. If you will not take it amiss I would ask you a question.

Chitra

You have permission.

Arjuna

What stern vow keeps you immured in this solitary temple, depriving all mortals of a vision of so much loveliness?

Chitra

I harbour a secret desire in my heart, for the fulfilment of which I offer daily prayers to Lord Shiva.

Arjuna

Alas, what can you desire, you who are the desire of the whole world! From the easternmost hill on whose summit the morning sun first prints his fiery foot to the end of the sunset land have I travelled. I have seen whatever is most precious, beautiful and great on the earth. My knowledge shall be yours, only say for what or for whom you seek.

Chitra

He whom I seek is known to all.

Arjuna

Indeed! Who may this favourite of the gods be, whose fame has captured your heart?

Chitra

Sprung from the highest of all royal houses, the greatest of all heroes is he.

Arjuna

Lady, offer not such wealth of beauty as is yours on the altar of false reputation. Spurious fame spreads from tongue to tongue like the fog of the early dawn before the sun rises. Tell me who in the highest of kingly lines is the supreme here?

Chitra

Hermit, you are jealous of other

men's fame. Do you not know that all over the world the royal house of the Kurus is the most famous?

Arjuna

The house of the Kurus!

Chitra

And have you never heard of the greatest name of that far-famed house?

Arjuna

From your own lips let me hear it.

Chitra

Arjuna, the conqueror of the world. I have culled from the mouths of the multitude that imperishable name and hidden it with care in my maiden heart. Hermit, why do you look perturbed? Has that name only a deceitful glitter? Say so, and I will not hesitate to break this casket of my heart and throw the false gem to the dust.

Arjuna

Be his name and fame, his bravery and prowess false or true, for mercy's sake do not banish him from your heart–for he kneels at your feet even now.

Chitra

You, Arjuna !

Arjuna

Yes, I am he, the love-hungered guest at your door.

Chitra

Then it is not true that Arjuna has taken a vow of chastity for twelve long years?

Arjuna

But you have dissolved my vow even as the moon dissolves the night's vow of obscurity.

Chitra

Oh, shame upon you! What have you seen in me that makes you false to yourself? Whom do you seek in these dark eyes, in these milk-white arms, if you are ready to pay for her the price of your probity? Not my true self, I know. Surely this cannot be love, this is not man's highest homage to woman! Alas, that this frail disguise, the body, should make one blind to the light of the deathless spirit! Yes, now indeed, I know, Arjuna, the fame of your heroic manhood is false.

Arjuna

Ah, I feel how vain is fame, the pride of prowess! Everything seems to me a dream. You alone are perfect; you are the wealth of the world, the end of all poverty, the goal of all efforts, the one woman! Others there are who can be but slowly known. While to see you for a moment is to see perfect completeness once and for ever.

Chitra

Alas, it is not I, not I, Arjuna! It is the deceit of a god. Go, go, my hero, go. Woo not falsehood, offer not your great heart to an illusion. Go.

SCENE III

Chitra

No, impossible. To face that fervent gaze that almost grasps you like clutching hands of the hungry spirit within; to feel his heart struggling to break its bounds urging its passionate cry through the entire body—and then to send him away like a beggar—no, impossible.

Enter MADANA *and* VASANTA.

Ah, god of love, what fearful flame is this with which thou hast enveloped me! I burn, and I burn whatever I touch.

Madana

I desire to know what happened last night.

Chitra

At evening I lay down on a grassy bed strewn with the petals of spring flowers, and recollected the wonderful praise of my beauty I had heard from Arjuna;—drinking drop by drop the honey that I had stored during the long day. The history of my past life like that of my former existences was forgotten. I felt like a flower, which has but a few fleeting hours to listen to all the humming flatteries and whispered murmurs of the woodlands and then must lower its eyes from the sky, bend its head and at a breath give itself up to the dust without a cry, thus ending the short story of a perfect moment that has neither past nor future.

Vasanta

A limitless life of glory can bloom and spend itself in a morning.

Madana

Like an endless meaning in the narrow span of a song.

Chitra

The southern breeze caressed me to sleep. From the flowering *Malati* bower overhead silent kisses dropped over my body. On my hair, my breast, my feet, each flower chose a bed to die on. I slept. And, suddenly in the depth of my sleep, I felt as if some intense eager look, like tapering fingers of flame, touched my slumbering body. I started up and saw the Hermit standing before me. The moon had moved to the west, peering through the leaves to espy this wonder of divine art wrought in a fragile human frame. The air was heavy with perfume; the silence of the night was vocal with the chirping of crickets; the reflections of the trees hung motionless in the lake; and with his staff in his hand he stood, tall and straight and still, like a forest tree. It seemed to me that I had, on opening my eyes, died to all realities of life and undergone a dream birth into a shadow land. Shame slipped to my feet like loosened clothes. I heard his call—"Beloved, my most beloved!" And all my forgotten lives united as one and responded to it. I said, "Take me, take all I am!" And I stretched out my arms to him. The moon set behind the trees. One curtain of darkness covered all. Heaven and earth, time and space, pleasure and pain, death and life merged together in an unbearable ecstasy. . . . With the first gleam of light, the first twitter of birds, I rose up and sat leaning on my left arm. He lay asleep with a vague smile about his lips like the crescent moon in the morning. The rosy red glow of the dawn fell upon his noble forehead. I sighed and stood up. I drew together the leafy lianas to screen the streaming sun from his face. I looked about me and saw the same old earth. I remembered what I used to be, and ran and ran like a deer afraid of her own shadow, through the forest path strewn with *shephali* flowers. I found a lonely nook, and sitting down covered my face with both hands, and tried to weep and cry. But no tears came to my eyes.

Madana

Alas, thou daughter of mortals! I stole from the divine storehouse the fragrant wine of heaven, filled with it one earthly night to the brim, and placed it in thy hand to drink—yet still I hear this cry of anguish!

Chitra [*bitterly*]

Who drank it? The rarest completion of life's desire, the first union of love was proffered to me, but was wrested from my grasp? This borrowed beauty, this falsehood that enwraps me, will slip from me taking with it the only monument of that sweet union, as the petals fall from an overblown flower; and the woman ashamed of her naked poverty will sit weeping day and night. Lord Love, this cursed appearance companions me like a demon robbing me of all the prizes of love—all the kisses for which my heart is athirst.

Madana

Alas, how vain thy single night had been! The barque of joy came in sight, but the waves would not let it touch the shore.

Chitra

Heaven came so close to my hand that I forgot for a moment that it had not reached me. But when I woke in the morning from my dream I found that my body had become my own rival. It is my hateful task to deck her every day, to send her to my beloved and see her caressed by him. O god, take back thy boon!

Madana

But if I take it from you how can you stand before your lover? To snatch away the cup from his lips when he has scarcely drained his first draught of pleasure, would not that be cruel? With what resentful anger he must regard thee then?

Chitra

That would be better far than this. I will reveal my true self to him, a nobler thing than this disguise. If he rejects it, if he spurns me and breaks my heart, I will bear even that in silence.

Vasanta

Listen to my advice. When with the advent of autumn the flowering season is over then comes the triumph of fruitage. A time will come of itself when the heat-cloyed bloom of the body will droop and Arjuna will gladly accept the abiding fruitful truth in thee. O child, go back to thy mad festival.

SCENE IV

Chitra

WHY do you watch me like that, my warrior?

Arjuna

I watch how you weave that garland. Skill and grace, the twin brother and sister, are dancing playfully on your finger-tips. I am watching and thinking.

Chitra

What are you thinking, sir?

Arjuna

I am thinking that you, with this same lightness of touch and sweetness, are weaving my days of exile into an immortal wreath, to crown me when I return home.

Chitra

Home! But this love is not for a home!

Arjuna

Not for a home?

Chitra

No. Never talk of that. Take to your home what is abiding and strong. Leave the little wild flower where it was born; leave it beautifully to die at the day's end among all fading blossoms and decaying leaves. Do not take it to your palace hall to fling it on the stony floor which knows no pity for things that fade and are forgotten.

Arjuna

Is ours that kind of love?

Chitra

Yes, no other! Why regret it? That which was meant for idle days should never outlive them. Joy turns into pain when the door by which it should depart is shut against it. Take it and keep it as long as it lasts. Let not the satiety of your evening claim more than the desire of your morning could earn. . . . The day is done. Put this garland on. I am tired. Take me in your arms, my love. Let all vain bickerings of discontent die away at the sweet meeting of our lips.

Arjuna

Hush! Listen, my beloved, the sound of prayer bells from the distant village temple steals upon the evening air across the silent trees!

SCENE V

Vasania

I CANNOT keep pace with thee, my friend! I am tired. It is a hard task to keep alive the fire thou hast kindled. Sleep overtakes me, the fan drops from my hand, and cold ashes cover the glow of the fire. I start up again from my slumber and with all my might rescue the weary flame. But this can go on no longer.

Madana

I know, thou art as fickle as a child. Ever restless is thy play in heaven and on earth. Things that thou for days buildest up with endless detail thou dost shatter in a moment without regret. But this work of ours is nearly finished. Pleasure-winged days fly fast, and the year, almost at its end, swoons in rapturous bliss.

SCENE VI

Arjuna

I WOKE in the morning and found that my dreams had distilled a gem. I have no casket to inclose it, no king's crown whereon to fix it, no chain from which to hang it, and yet have not the heart to throw it away. My Kshatriya's right arm, idly occupied in holding it, forgets its duties.

Enter CHITRA.

Chitra

Tell me your thoughts, sir!

Arjuna

My mind is busy with thoughts of hunting to-day. See, how the rain pours in torrents and fiercely beats upon the hillside. The dark shadow of the clouds hangs heavily over the forest, and the swollen stream, like reckless youth, overleaps all barriers with mocking laughter. On such rainy days we five brothers would go to the Chitraka forest to chase wild beasts. Those were glad times. Our hearts danced to the drumbeat of rumbling clouds. The woods resounded with the screams of peacocks. Timid deer could not hear our approaching steps for the patter of rain and the noise of waterfalls; the leopards would leave their tracks on the wet earth, betraying their lairs. Our sport over, we dared each other to swim across turbulent streams on our way back home. The restless spirit is on me. I long to go hunting.

Chitra

First run down the quarry you are now following. Are you quite certain that the enchanted deer you pursue must needs be caught? No, not yet. Like a dream the wild creature eludes you when it seems most nearly yours. Look how the wind is chased by the mad rain that discharges a thousand arrows after it. Yet it goes free and unconquered. Our sport is like that, my love! You give chase to the fleet-footed spirit of beauty, aiming at her every dart you have in your hands. Yet this magic deer runs ever free and untouched.

Arjuna

My love, have you no home where kind hearts are waiting for your return? A home which you once made sweet with your gentle service and whose light went out when you left it for this wilderness?

Chitra

Why these questions? Are the hours of unthinking pleasure over? Do you not know that I am no more than what you see before you? For me there is no vista beyond. The dew that hangs on the tip of a Kinsuka petal has neither name nor destination. It offers no answer to any question. She whom you love is like that perfect bead of dew.

Arjuna

Has she no tie with the world? Can she be merely like a fragment of heaven dropped on the earth through the carelessness of a wanton god?

Chitra

Yes.

Arjuna

Ah, that is why I always seem about to lose you. My heart is unsatisfied, my mind knows no peace. Come closer to me, unattainable one! Surrender yourself to the bonds of name and home and parentage. Let my heart feel you on all sides and live with you in the peaceful security of love.

Chitra

Why this vain effort to catch and keep the tints of the clouds, the dance of the waves, the smell of the flowers?

Arjuna

Mistress mine, do not hope to pacify love with airy nothings. Give me something to clasp, something that can last longer than pleasure, that can endure even through suffering.

Chitra

Hero mine, the year is not yet full, and you are tired already! Now I know that it is Heaven's blessing that has made the flower's term of life short. Could this body of mine have drooped and died with the flowers of last spring it surely would have died with honour. Yet, its days are numbered, my love. Spare it not, press it dry of honey, for fear your beggar's heart come back to it again and again with unsated desire, like a thirsty bee when summer blossoms lie dead in the dust.

SCENE VII

Madana

TO-NIGHT is thy last night.

Vasanta

The loveliness of your body will return to-morrow to the inexhaustible stores of the spring. The ruddy tint of thy lips freed from the memory of Arjuna's kisses, will bud anew as a pair of fresh *asoka* leaves, and the soft, white glow of thy skin will be born again in a hundred fragrant jasmine flowers.

Chitra

O gods, grant me this my prayer! To-night, in its last hour let my beauty flash its brightest, like the final flicker of a dying flame.

Madana

Thou shalt have thy wish.

SCENE VIII

Villagers

WHO will protect us now?

Arjuna

Why, by what danger are you threatened?

Villagers

The robbers are pouring from the northern hills like a mountain flood to devastate our village.

Arjuna

Have you in this kingdom no warden?

Villagers

Princess Chitra was the terror of all evil doers. While she was in this happy land we feared natural deaths, but had no other fears. Now she has gone on a pilgrimage, and none knows where to find her.

Arjuna

Is the warden of this country a woman?

Villagers

Yes, she is our father and mother in one.

[*Exeunt.*

Enter CHITRA.

Chitra

Why are you sitting all alone?

Arjuna

I am trying to imagine what kind of woman Princess Chitra may be. I hear so many stories of her from all sorts of men.

Chitra

Ah, but she is not beautiful. She has no such lovely eyes as mine, dark as death. She can pierce any target she will, but not our hero's heart.

Arjuna

They say that in valour she is a man, and a woman in tenderness.

Chitra

That, indeed, is her greatest misfortune. When a woman is merely a woman; when she winds herself round and round men's hearts with her smiles and sobs and services and caressing endearments; then she is happy. Of what use to her are learning and great achievements? Could you have seen her only yesterday in the court of the Lord Shiva's temple by the forest path, you would have passed by without deigning to look at her. But have you grown so weary of woman's beauty that you seek in her for a man's strength?

With green leaves wet from the spray of the foaming waterfall, I have made our noonday bed in a cavern dark as night. There the cool of the soft green mosses thick on the black and dripping stone kisses your eyes to sleep. Let me guide you thither.

Arjuna

Not to-day, beloved.

Chitra

Why not to-day?

Arjuna

I have heard that a horde of robbers has neared the plains. Needs must I go and prepare my weapons to protect the frightened villagers.

Chitra

You need have no fear for them. Before she started on her pilgrimage, Princess Chitra had set strong guards at all the frontier passes.

Arjuna

Yet permit me for a short while to set about a Kshatriya's work. With new glory will I ennoble this idle arm, and make of it a pillow more worthy of your head.

Chitra

What if I refuse to let you go, if I keep you entwined in my arms? Would you rudely snatch yourself free and leave me? Go then! But you must know that the liana, once broken in two, never joins again. Go, if your thirst is quenched. But, if not, then remember that the goddess of pleasure is fickle, and waits for no man. Sit for a while, my lord! Tell me what uneasy thoughts tease you. Who occupied your mind to-day? Is it Chitra?

Arjuna

Yes, it is Chitra. I wonder in fulfilment of what vow she has gone on her pilgrimage. Of what could she stand in need?

Chitra

Her needs? Why, what has she ever had, the unfortunate creature? Her very qualities are as prison walls, shutting her woman's heart in a bare cell. She is obscured, she is unfulfilled. Her womanly love must content itself dressed in rags; beauty is denied her. She is like the spirit of a cheerless morning, sitting upon the stony mountain peak, all her light blotted out by dark clouds. Do not ask me of her life. It will never sound sweet to man's ear.

Arjuna

I am eager to learn all about her. I am like a traveller come to a strange city at midnight. Domes and towers and garden-trees look vague and shadowy, and the dull moan of the sea comes fitfully through the silence of sleep. Wistfully he waits for the morning to reveal to him all the strange wonders. Oh, tell me her story.

Chitra

What more is there to tell ?

Arjuna

I seem to see her, in my mind's eye, riding on a white horse, proudly holding the reins in her left hand, and in her right a bow, and like the Goddess of Victory dispensing glad hope all round her. Like a watchful lioness she protects the litter at her dugs with a fierce love. Woman's arms, though adorned with naught but unfettered strength, are beautiful! My heart is restless, fair one, like a serpent reviving from his long winter's sleep. Come, let us both race on swift horses side by side, like twin orbs of light sweeping through space. Out from this slumbrous prison of green gloom, this dank, dense cover of perfumed intoxication, choking breath.

Chitra

Arjuna, tell me true, if, now at once, by some magic I could shake myself free from this voluptuous softness, this timid bloom of beauty shrinking from the rude and healthy touch of the world, and fling it from my body like borrowed clothes, would you be able to bear it? If I stand up straight and strong with the strength of a daring heart spurning the wiles and arts of twining weakness, if I hold my head high like a tall young mountain fir, no longer trailing in the dust like a liana, shall I then appeal to man's eye? No, no, you could not endure it. It is better that I should keep spread about me all the dainty playthings of fugitive youth, and wait for you in patience. When it pleases you to return, I will smilingly pour out for you the wine of pleasure in the cup of this beauteous body. When you are tired and satiated with this wine, you can go to work or play; and when I grow old I will accept humbly and gratefully whatever corner is left for me. Would it please your heroic soul if the playmate of the night aspired to be the helpmeet of the day, if the left arm learnt to share the burden of the proud right arm?

Arjuna

I never seem to know you aright. You seem to me like a goddess hidden within a golden image. I cannot touch you, I cannot pay you my dues in return for your priceless gifts. Thus my love is incomplete. Sometimes in the enigmatic depth of your sad look, in your playful words mocking at their own meaning, I gain glimpses of a being trying to rend asunder the languorous grace of her body, to emerge in a chaste fire of pain through a vaporous veil of smiles. Illusion is the first appearance of Truth. She advances towards her lover in disguise. But a time comes when she throws off her ornaments and veils and stands clothed in naked dignity. I grope for that ultimate *you*, that bare simplicity of truth.

Why these tears, my love? Why

cover your face with your hands? Have I pained you, my darling? Forget what I said. I will be content with the present. Let each separate moment of beauty come to me like a bird of mystery from its unseen nest in the dark bearing a message of music. Let me for ever sit with my hope on the brink of its realization, and thus end my days.

favour your face with your smiles? Have I pained you by my [illegible]? I will be content with the present. Let each separate moment of beauty come to me like a bird of mystery from its unseen nest in the dark bearing a message of music. Let me for ever sit with my hopes on the brink of their realization, and thus pass my days.

SCENE IX

CHITRA *and* ARJUNA

Chitra [*cloaked*]

MY lord, has the cup been drained to the last drop? Is this, indeed, the end? No, when all is done something still remains, and that is my last sacrifice at your feet.

I brought from the garden of heaven flowers of incomparable beauty with which to worship you, god of my heart. If the rites are over, if the flowers have faded, let me throw them out of the temple [*unveiling in her original male attire.*] Now, look at your worshipper with gracious eyes.

I am not beautifully perfect as the flowers with which I worshipped. I have many flaws and blemishes. I am a traveller in the great world-path, my garments are dirty, and my feet are bleeding with thorns. Where should I achieve flower-beauty, the unsullied loveliness of a moment's life? The gift that I proudly bring you is the heart of a woman. Here have all pains and joys gathered, the hopes and fears and shames of a daughter of the dust; here love springs up struggling toward immortal life. Herein lies an imperfection which yet is noble and grand. If the flower-service is finished, my master, accept *this* as your servant for the days to come!

I am Chitra, the king's daughter. Perhaps you will remember the day when a woman came to you in the temple of Shiva, her body loaded with ornaments and finery. That shameless woman came to court you as though she were a man. You rejected her; you did well. My lord, I am that woman. She was my disguise. Then by the boon of gods I obtained for a year the most radiant form that a mortal ever wore, and wearied my hero's heart with the burden of that deceit. Most surely I am not that woman.

I am Chitra. No goddess to be worshipped, nor yet the object of common pity to be brushed aside like a moth with indifference. If you deign to keep me by your side in the path of danger and daring, if you allow me to share the great duties of your life, then you will know my true self. If your babe, whom I am nourishing in my womb, be born a son, I shall myself teach him to be a second Arjuna, and send him to you when the time comes, and then at last you will truly know me. To-day

I can only offer you Chitra, the daughter of a king.

Arjuna

Beloved, my life is full.

THE END